The Reptile Ball

by Jacqueline K. Ogburn pictures by John O'Brien

Dial Books for Young Readers · New York

Published by Dial Books for Young Readers
A Division of Penguin Books USA Inc.
375 Hudson Street
New York, New York 10014

Designed by Julie Rauer
Printed in Hong Kong
First Edition
1 3 5 7 9 10 8 6 4 2

Library of Congress Cataloging in Publication Data
Ogburn, Jacqueline K.
The reptile ball/by Jacqueline K. Ogburn; pictures by John O'Brien.—1st ed.
p. cm.
Summary: Lighthearted poems recount how the creatures
slither and crawl at the Reptile Ball.
ISBN 0-8037-1731-8. —ISBN 0-8037-1732-6 (library)
1. Reptiles—Juvenile poetry. 2. Amphibians—Juvenile poetry.
3. Balls (Parties)—Juvenile poetry. 4. Children's poetry, American.
[1. Reptiles—Poetry. 2. Amphibians—Poetry. 3. Balls (Parties)—Poetry.
4. American poetry.] I. O'Brien, John, date, ill. II. Title.
PS3565.G33R46 1997b 811'.54—dc20 96-9628 CIP AC

The art for this book was created using concentrated watercolors and
assorted dyes. It was then color-separated and reproduced
as red, blue, yellow, and black halftones.

To Emily Harper Deahl

J.K.O.

To Tess

J.O.

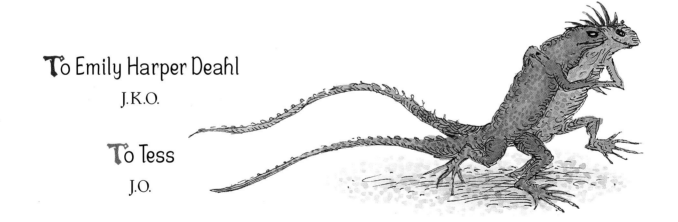

The Reptile Ball

On the autumn night of the Hunter's Moon,
In a secret, elegant underground room,
Collect the creatures who slither and crawl
In a creepy display called the Reptile Ball.

The Dining Hall

Forty cooks worked forty days,
preparing the Reptile Ball buffets.
Arranged on platters with precision and haste,
a dish to delight each cold-blooded taste.

    Fried ant squares and
        beetle-wing tarts,
    Gizzard gumbo with
        octopus hearts.
    Caterpillar soup and
        roasted rat tails,
    Skunkwort leaves
        garnished with snails.
    Brussels sprouts in
        fish-eye sauce,
    Slugs flambé on
        Spanish moss.
    Butterfly crisps,
        honey-dipped bees,
    Stump-water shakes
        sprinkled with fleas.

The tables are set with china so fine,
next to each place a discreet little sign.
"For the comfort of all, we make this request:
Please refrain from eating the other guests."

Procession of the Komodo Dragons

Fine, wise, courtly pace,
Colored silk over dark scales,
Slow, stern dragon grace.

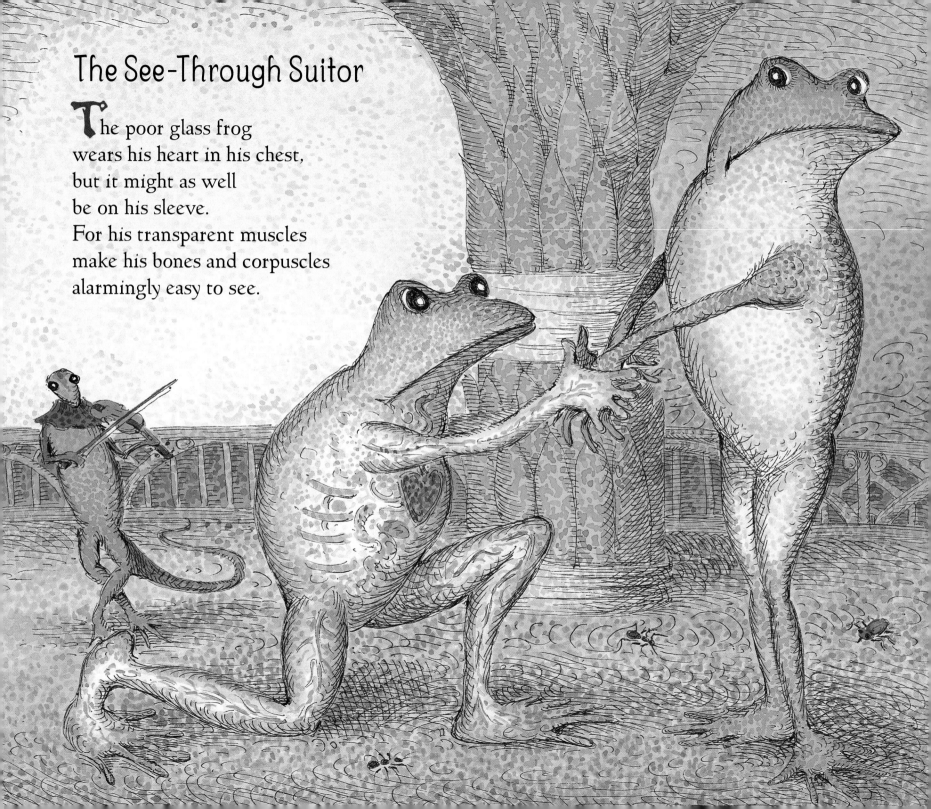

The See-Through Suitor

The poor glass frog
wears his heart in his chest,
but it might as well
be on his sleeve.
For his transparent muscles
make his bones and corpuscles
alarmingly easy to see.

Horned Toad Two-Step

Old step, new step
Horned Toad two-step
How do you do step
Fine and you? step
Kick up your shoe step
Hop on through step
Can't stay blue step
Shout "Yah-hoo!" step
Old step, new step
Horned Toad two-step!

Ssa-Ssa-Ssamba

Snakes all shake in the Ssa-Ssa-Ssamba,
Heeding the plea of the Anaconda,
Pit Vipers strike their slim marimbas,
Glide at the side of the giant Mambas,
Rattlesnakes clatter: Tcha-che-cha-cha,
Snakes all shake in the Ssa-Ssa-Ssamba!

The Perfect Wallflower

She's pink by the punch bowl,
    Green by the bower,
Never has there been
    A more perfect wallflower.

Poor shy chameleon,
    Blending with the wall,
The partner that she longs for
    Can't see her at all.

Wistfully he gazes,
    Wondering what to do,
Instead of one wallflower,
    Now there are two.

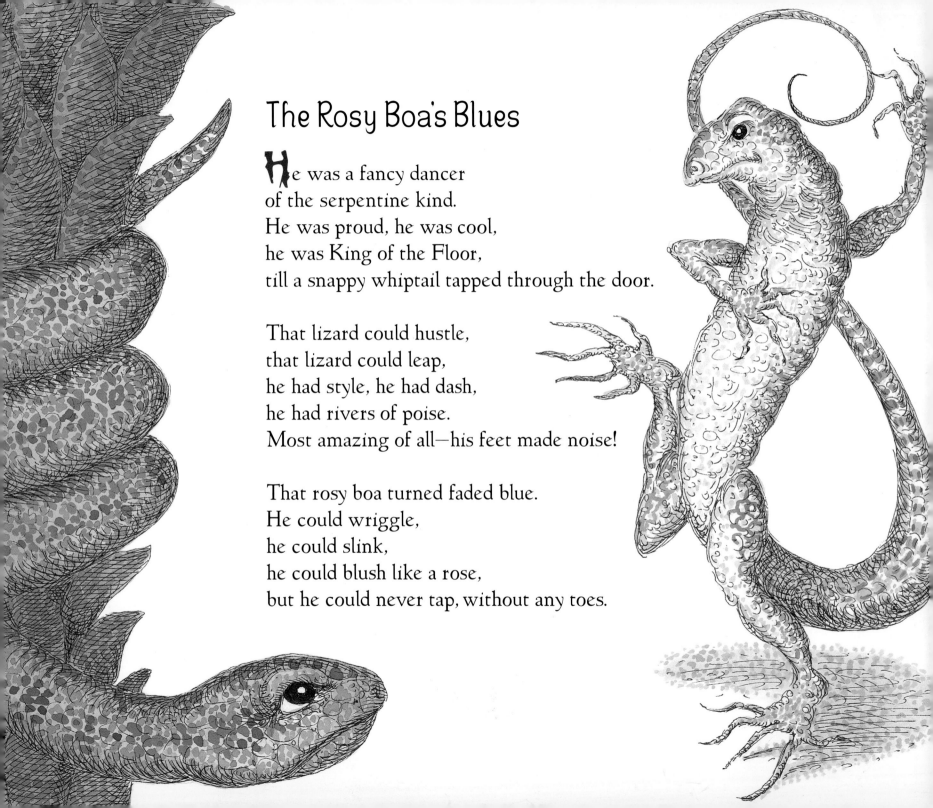

The Rosy Boa's Blues

He was a fancy dancer
of the serpentine kind.
He was proud, he was cool,
he was King of the Floor,
till a snappy whiptail tapped through the door.

That lizard could hustle,
that lizard could leap,
he had style, he had dash,
he had rivers of poise.
Most amazing of all—his feet made noise!

That rosy boa turned faded blue.
He could wriggle,
he could slink,
he could blush like a rose,
but he could never tap, without any toes.

Hissing
Casanova

Tongue flick
Step quick
Coy miss
Hand kiss
Tail curl
Fast twirl
Lazy wink
Fickle skink
New dance
New romance.

Gila Monster March

Gilas come marching, two by two.
Gilas are black and pink and blue.
    Gilas are rowdy,
    Gilas are rude.
Gilas don't dance—
They've come for the food.

A Peculiar Pair

A tree frog waltzed through the hall
with a turtle, both ancient and tall.
    In the midst of their motion,
    he explained his devotion:
"For your eyes are so exquisitely small."

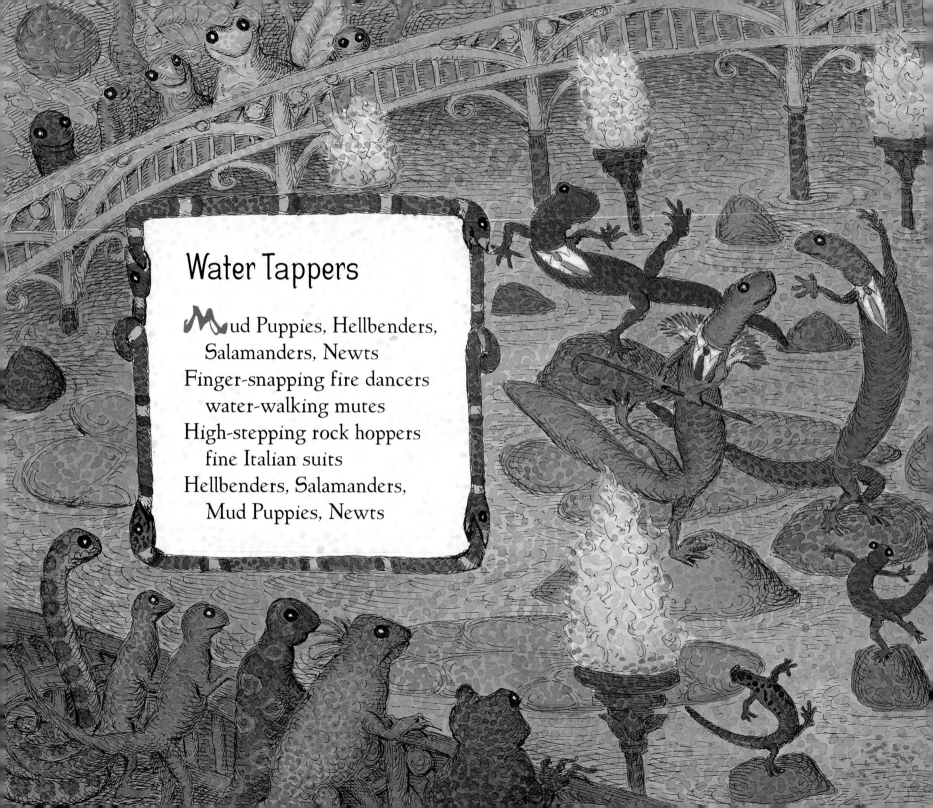

Water Tappers

Mud Puppies, Hellbenders,
　Salamanders, Newts
Finger-snapping fire dancers
　water-walking mutes
High-stepping rock hoppers
　fine Italian suits
Hellbenders, Salamanders,
　Mud Puppies, Newts

The Toad and Frog Reel

Bow to your partner, pretty as pie,
Wink your bright and bulgy eye.

Frogs leap high and toads hop low,
Slap the floor with heel and toe.

Snap your tongue at a ceiling fly,
Promenade your partner, sweet and shy.

Tree frogs trill and bullfrogs chug,
Everybody grin as you cut the rug.

Now do-si-do and don't you roam,
All good amphibians jump on home.
All good amphibians jump on home.

Alligator Stomp

Suave Egyptian crocodiles
Crack wicked, toothy smiles,
When their cousins from the swamp
Start the Alligator Stomp.
   Clomp!
Kin from Cairo and Decatur,
Both sides of the equator,
Grinning leatherbacks thomp
In the Alligator Stomp.
   Clomp!
Smaller dancers have to run
From the table-smashing fun
Of the tail-swinging romp
Called the Alligator Stomp.
   CLOMP!

The Last Dance

One final turn beneath the setting moon,
the orchestra plays a bittersweet tune.
Day comes creeping, the Ball is done.
Dancers drift home to sleep in the sun.

Glossary

 **Alligator:** A large reptile ranging from six to eighteen feet in length that lives near fresh water; closely related to the crocodile.

 **Anaconda:** A type of boa constrictor that lives in South America and can grow up to thirty-six feet long.

 **Bullfrog:** A large frog with a deep voice.

 Chameleon: A tree-dwelling lizard that lives in Africa. It can change color and blend in with its surroundings. Its eyes are cone-shaped and can swivel backward.

 **Chuckwalla:** A large southwestern American lizard with baggy skin that it can inflate for protection.

 **Crocodile:** A large reptile ranging from five to twenty-five feet in length that lives near fresh water; closely related to the alligator.

 **Frog:** An amphibian found throughout the world.

 **Galápagos giant tortoise:** One of the largest land tortoises, found only on the Galápagos Islands.

 Gecko: A small lizard found throughout the world. Some have special feet that enable them to walk up walls.

 **Gila monster:** A poisonous lizard found in the southwestern United States and Mexico, with scales like woven beads.

 **Glass frog:** A small Central American frog that lives in trees and has translucent skin that reveals the bones and blood vessels.

 **Goanna:** An Australian lizard.

 **Hellbender:** A North American giant salamander that grows up to twenty-nine inches long and lives in fresh water.

 **Horned toad:** Not really a toad, but a lizard, found in the southwestern United States, with a spiky tail, sides, and head.

Note: Some of these creatures appear in the art but not in the text.

Iguana: A crested lizard, found mostly in North and South America.

Komodo dragon: The largest living lizard, reaching up to ten feet in length; found on the Pacific island of Komodo in Southeast Asia.

Mamba: A poisonous African snake.

Mud puppy: A North American salamander whose gills remain external even as an adult.

Newt: A small salamander that lives in North America and Europe.

Pit viper: Any one of several kinds of poisonous snakes that have a "pit" between their eyes and nostrils that senses heat.

Python: A large, nonpoisonous African and Indian snake that constricts its prey.

Rattlesnake: A type of pit viper found in North America that has "rattles" on its tail.

Rosy boa: A North American constrictor that is a dusty rose color.

Salamander: An amphibian that looks like a slimy lizard and lives in North America and Europe. In European folklore, salamanders are associated with fire.

Skink: A small lizard found throughout the world.

Toad: An amphibian, similar to frogs, with rough skin.

Tree frog: Any one of several kinds of tiny tree-dwelling frogs that is found throughout the world, sometimes brightly colored with a high voice.

Whiptail: A lizard with a long thin tail that lives in North and South America.